MAX EXPLAINS EVERYTHING
Soccer Expert

STACY McANULTY

ILLUSTRATED BY
DEBORAH HOCKING

putnam

G. P. PUTNAM'S SONS

For Henry and all the kiddos in
the Kernersville Soccer Association—S.McA.

For my coaches through the years. Thanks for all the rainy
practices, late night games, and lessons in life skills—D.H.

G. P. PUTNAM'S SONS
an imprint of Penguin Random House LLC
375 Hudson Street
New York, NY 10014

Library of Congress Cataloging-in-Publication Data
Names: McAnulty, Stacy, author. | Hocking, Deborah, illustrator.
Title: Max explains everything : soccer expert / Stacy McAnulty ; illustrated by Deborah Hocking.
Description: New York, NY : G. P. Putnam's Sons, [2019]
Summary: Nearly three weeks after starting to play soccer, Max shares his "expert" knowledge
of clothing, warm-ups, cheering for his teammates—everything but actually kicking the ball.
Identifiers: LCCN 2017056631 | ISBN 9781101996409 (hc) | ISBN 9781101996416 (epub fxl cpb) |
ISBN 9781101996423 (kf8/kindle) | Subjects: | CYAC: Soccer—Fiction. | Behavior—Fiction. |
Humorous stories. Classification: LCC PZ7.M47825255 Maz 2019 | DDC [E]—dc23
LC record available at https://lccn.loc.gov/2017056631

Manufactured in China by RR Donnelley Asia Printing Solutions Ltd.
ISBN 9781101996409
10 9 8 7 6 5 4 3 2 1

Design by Marikka Tamura. Text set in Gotham Medium.
The illustrations were created with gouache and colored pencil
on Arches watercolor paper, then digitally manipulated.

I know a lot about soccer.
I've been playing it for a long time
—almost three weeks.

Practice is fun. But game days are the best.

You wear special shoes called cleats.

And a shirt with your lucky number. (You know it's lucky because it's on *your* shirt.)

And battle armor on your legs. I wish we got helmets and shields too.

Max, ready to get out there and kick that ball?

Make sure you warm up before the game.

Stretch.

Twirl.

Somersault.

In the huddle, Coach will tell you that winning is not important.

The game starts when the ref blows the whistle.

He's the guy in yellow, and he has a whistle.

(You should not bring your own whistle.)

Other stuff you should not bring to a soccer game:

Crayons.

A blanket (even if you just want to wear it as a cape).

Your seashell collection or dust bunny collection or any collection, really.

Sometimes there are dandelions and four-leaf clovers on the field.

I pull these out so no one gets distracted.

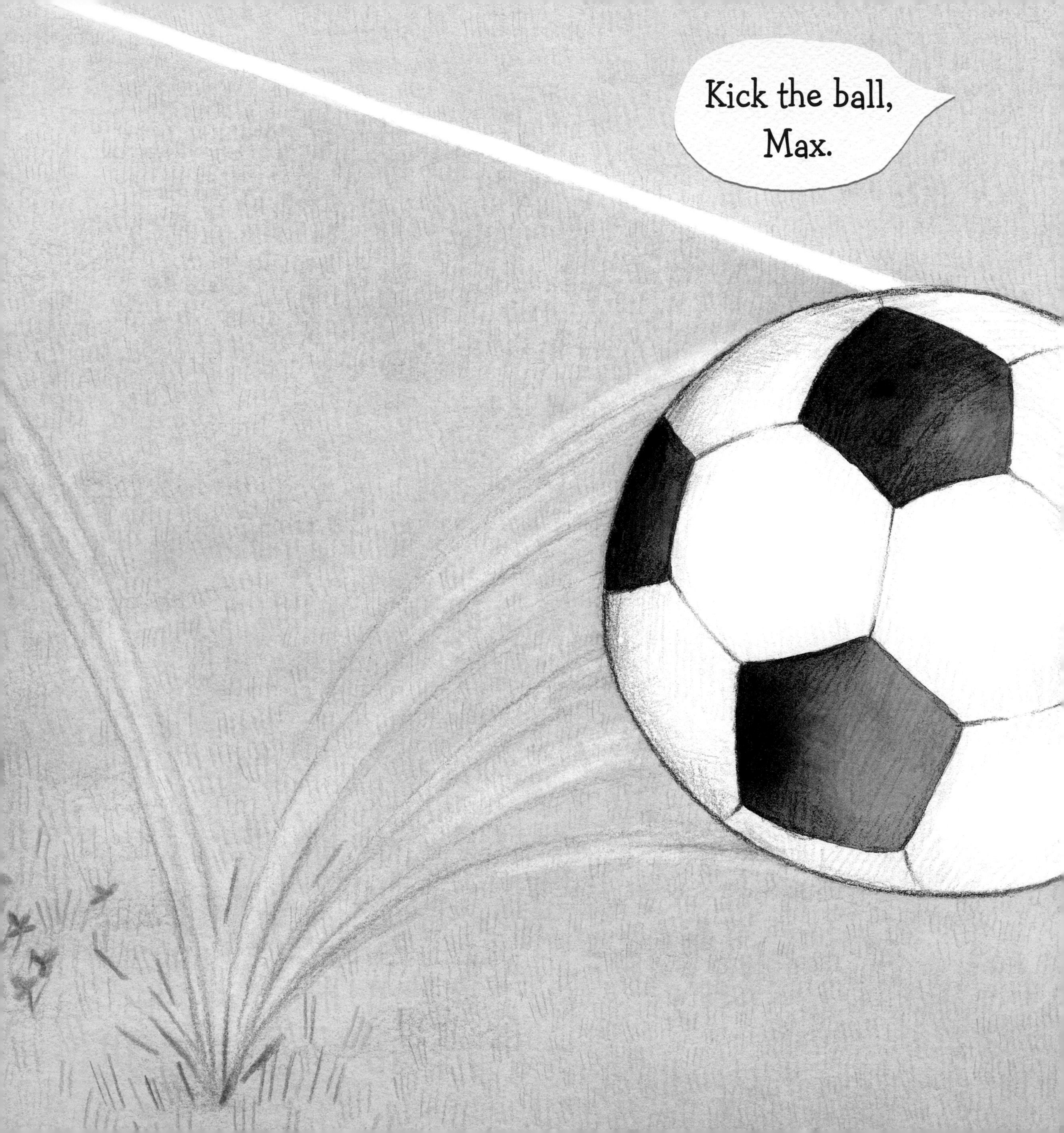
Kick the ball, Max.

And sometimes there are ladybugs and worms.
You should move these so they don't get hurt.

Thousands of fans come to the games, and they all take pictures.

I like to give them different poses.

Maybe one smiling.

And a serious one.

Let's take a picture of you kicking the ball.

And one with my teammates.

The clouds over the soccer field can be amazing.
I've seen an alligator, a toothbrush, and a diamond ring.

Nothing today.

Coach wants everyone to play. So sometimes you will sit on the side and cheer on your teammates.

When you go back in the game, you must be ready for anything.

Last week, a dog ran out on the field.

Come here, puppy.

Can we keep him, Mom?

In soccer, you can't use your hands to touch the ball. I've come up with other things to do with my hands so they don't get bored.

I wave at the fans.

I hide them in my shirt.

I play itsy-bitsy spider.

I feel like I'm forgetting
something important . . .

Something you have to do in soccer . . .

SNACK!

That's it. I can't believe I almost forgot.
You get a snack at the end.

Shake hands with the other team first.